Mommy
Loves
You!

For Jean and Al Ferris, EJ, Kerry, and for my mom, Naomi C Foster
—Helen Foster James

❀

For Rosie

— Petra Brown

Sleeping Bear Press™
2395 South Huron Parkway, Suite 200
Ann Arbor, MI 48104
www.sleepingbearpress.com

Printed and bound in the United States.

10 9 8 7 6 5 4 3 2 1

Library of Congress Cataloging-in-Publication Data on file.

ISBN: 978-158536-941-6

This book is presented to:

_____

On this day:

_____

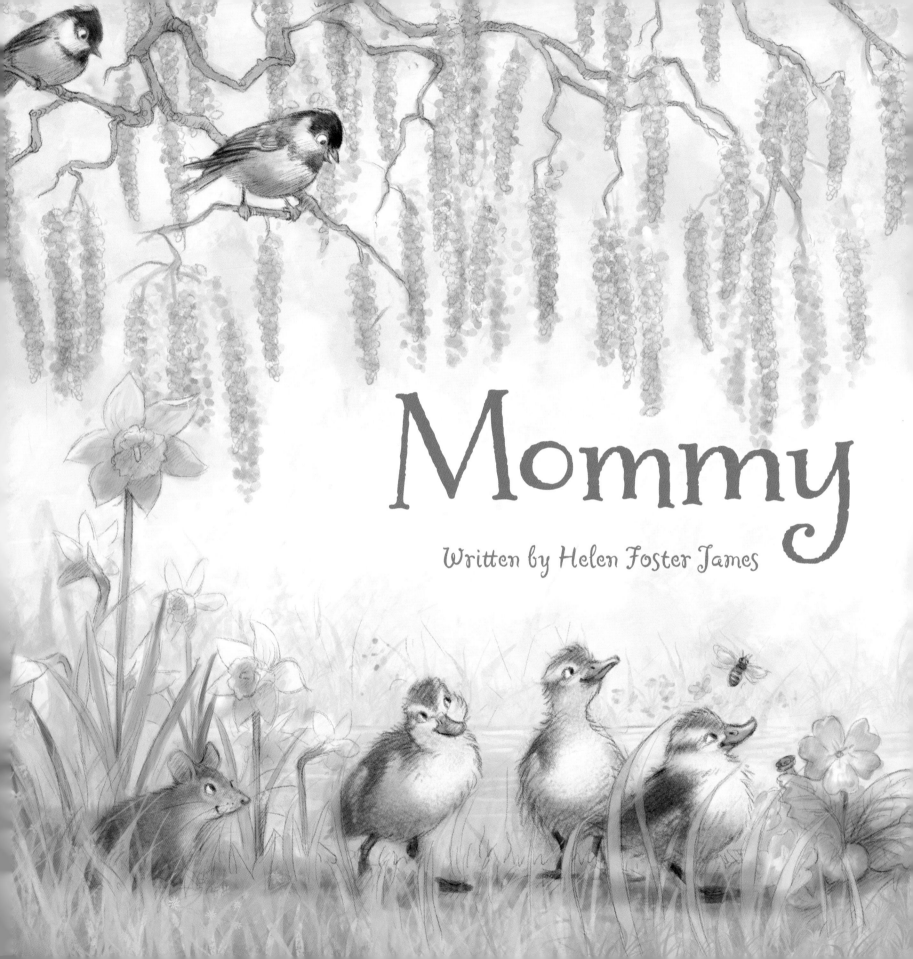

Mommy

Written by Helen Foster James

Loves You!

Illustrated by Petra Brown

Your mommy loves you,
my bunny, I do.

Millions of kisses
I have just for you.

My heart's full of love
that blossoms and grows

from your little nose
to those teensy toes.

You are my moonbeam,
my star in the sky.

My hopes and my heart,
my cute honey pie.

On tippy-tiptoes,
you'll reach when you're small.

Hug-a-bug bunny,
I'll watch you grow tall.

Dream big, bunny-cakes.
Jump rope in the sun.

Sing songs with your friends.
Be happy, have fun.

Dance and discover
and wish on a star.

Be silly and kind–
be just who you are.

You made me a mom,
and I'm glad you're here

to share loads of love
each day of the year.

In all this big world,
my sweet little pea,

you are so special,
so precious to me.

A Special Letter to My Child

_____

_____

_____

_____

_____

_____

_____

_____

With Love, _____

Paste a picture of Mommy
and child here.